THE ... IMPORTANT PEA

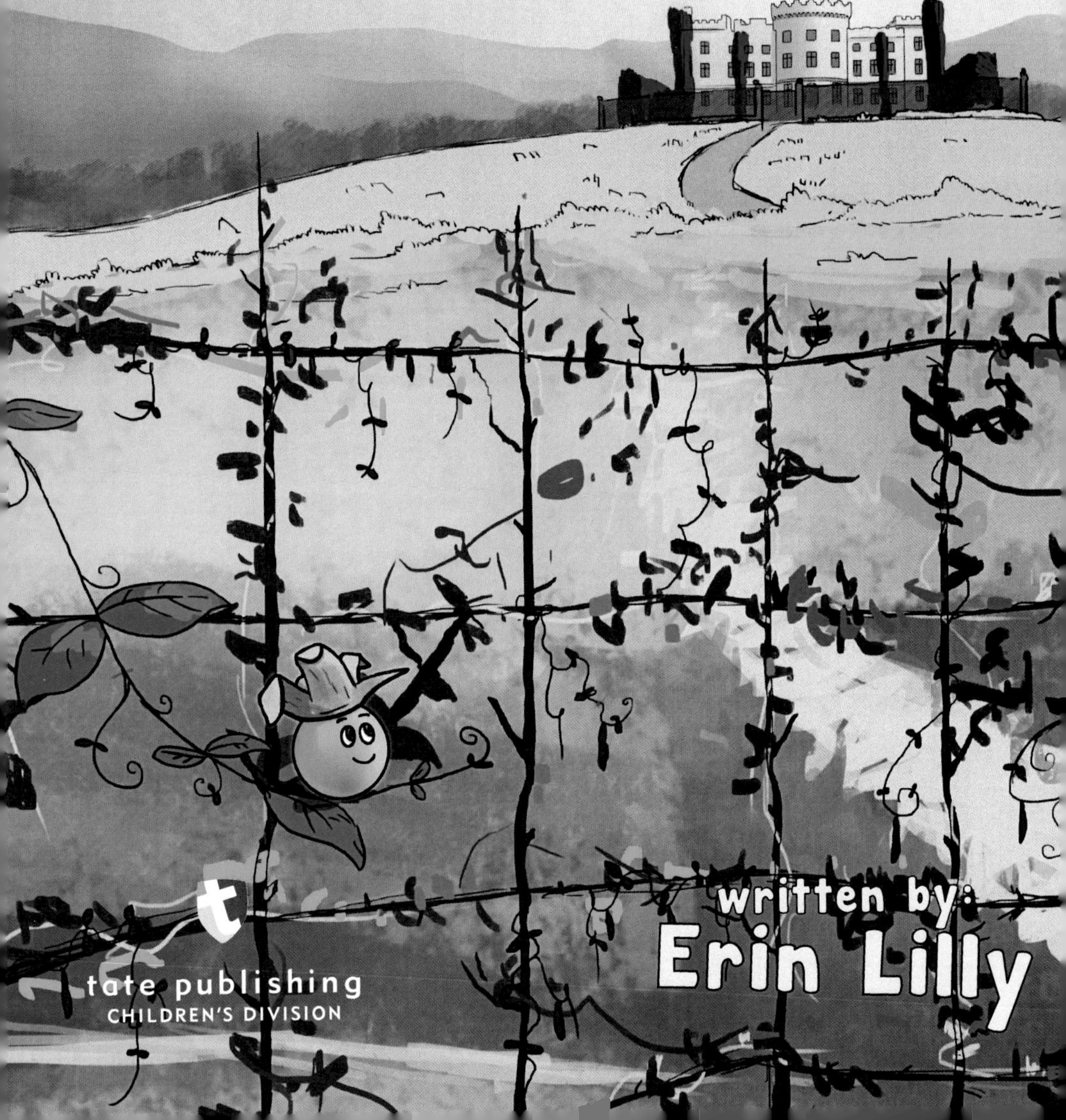

written by:
Erin Lilly

tate publishing
CHILDREN'S DIVISION

This title is also available as a Tate Out Loud product. Visit www.tatepublishing.com for more information.

Published by Tate Publishing & Enterprises, LLC
127 E. Trade Center Terrace | Mustang, Oklahoma 73064 USA
1.888.361.9473 | www.tatepublishing.com

Tate Publishing is committed to excellence in the publishing industry. The company reflects the philosophy established by the founders, based on Psalm 68:11,
"The Lord gave the word and great was the company of those who published it."

Cover and interior design by Eileen Cueno
Illustrations by Kenneth rede Rikimaru

Published in the United States of America

ISBN: 978-1-68164-925-2
Juvenile Fiction / Fairy Tales & Folklore / Adaptations
15.07.03

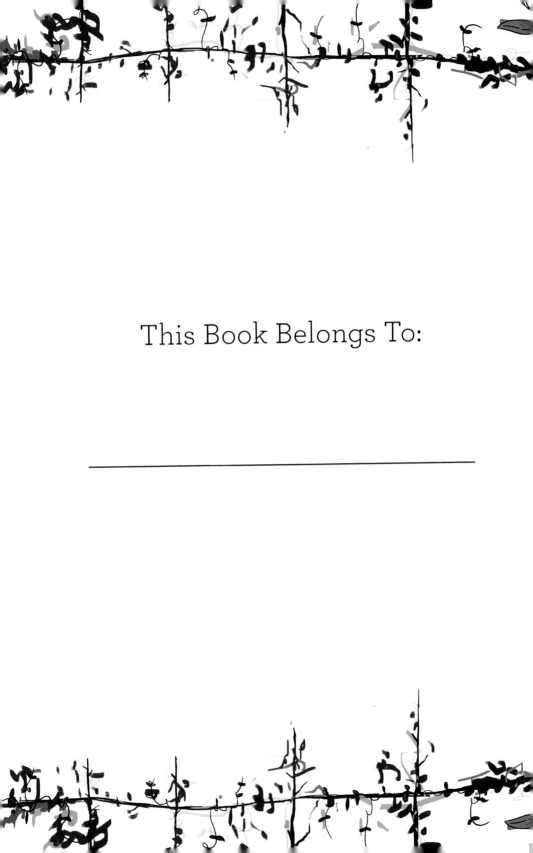

This Book Belongs To:

_____

To Molly Engle for telling me to write this,
or she was going to,
and to my family for believing in me.

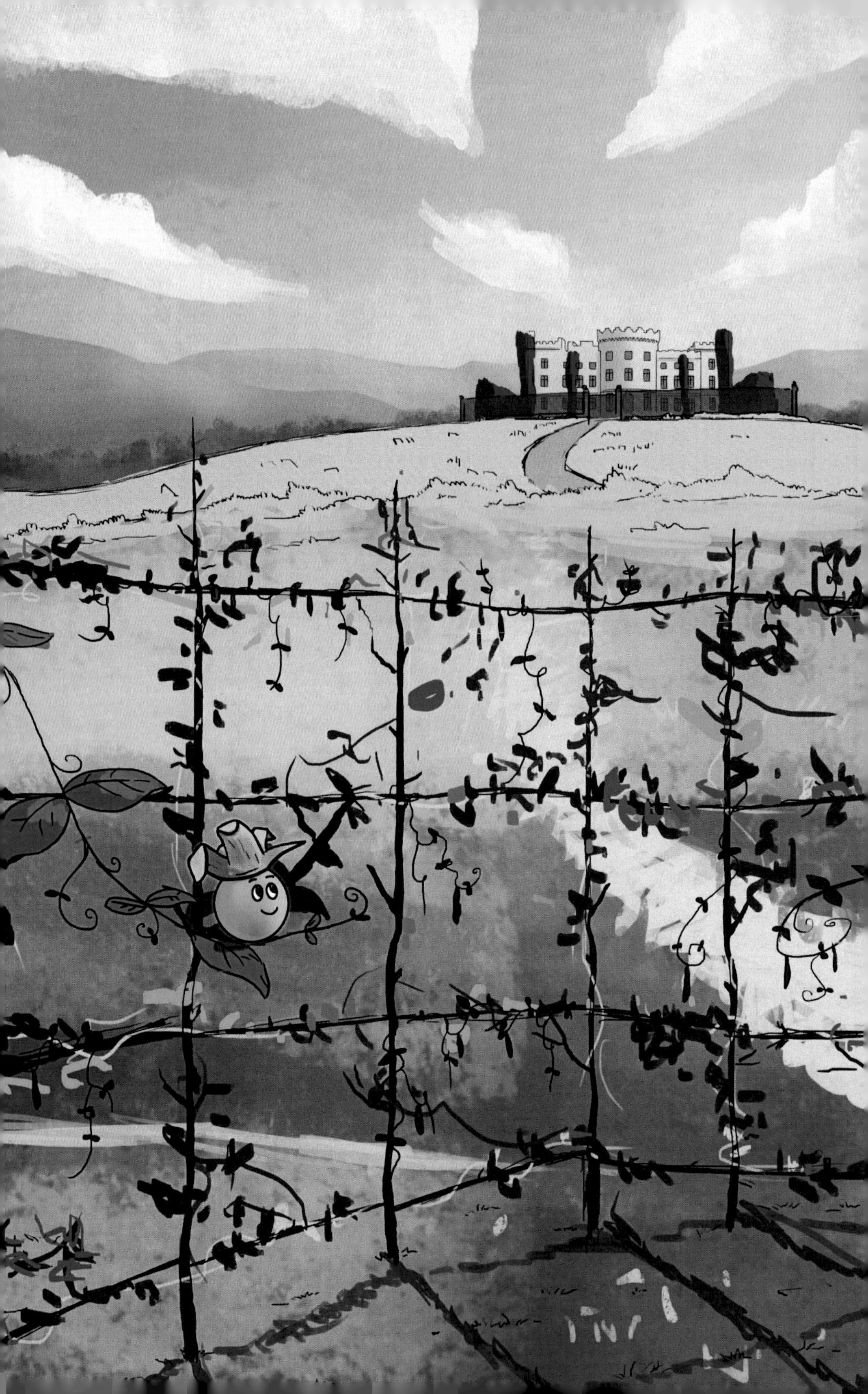

Once upon a time there was a prince
that wanted to marry a princess—

"Well, don't most princes want to marry a princess? Besides this story isn't about that, well, sort of, it's about me and how I helped a prince find his princess and became the most important pea of all time. I'm sure you know the story of *The Princess and the Pea*, but you don't know it from my side. Okay, sorry, Narrator, you may continue."

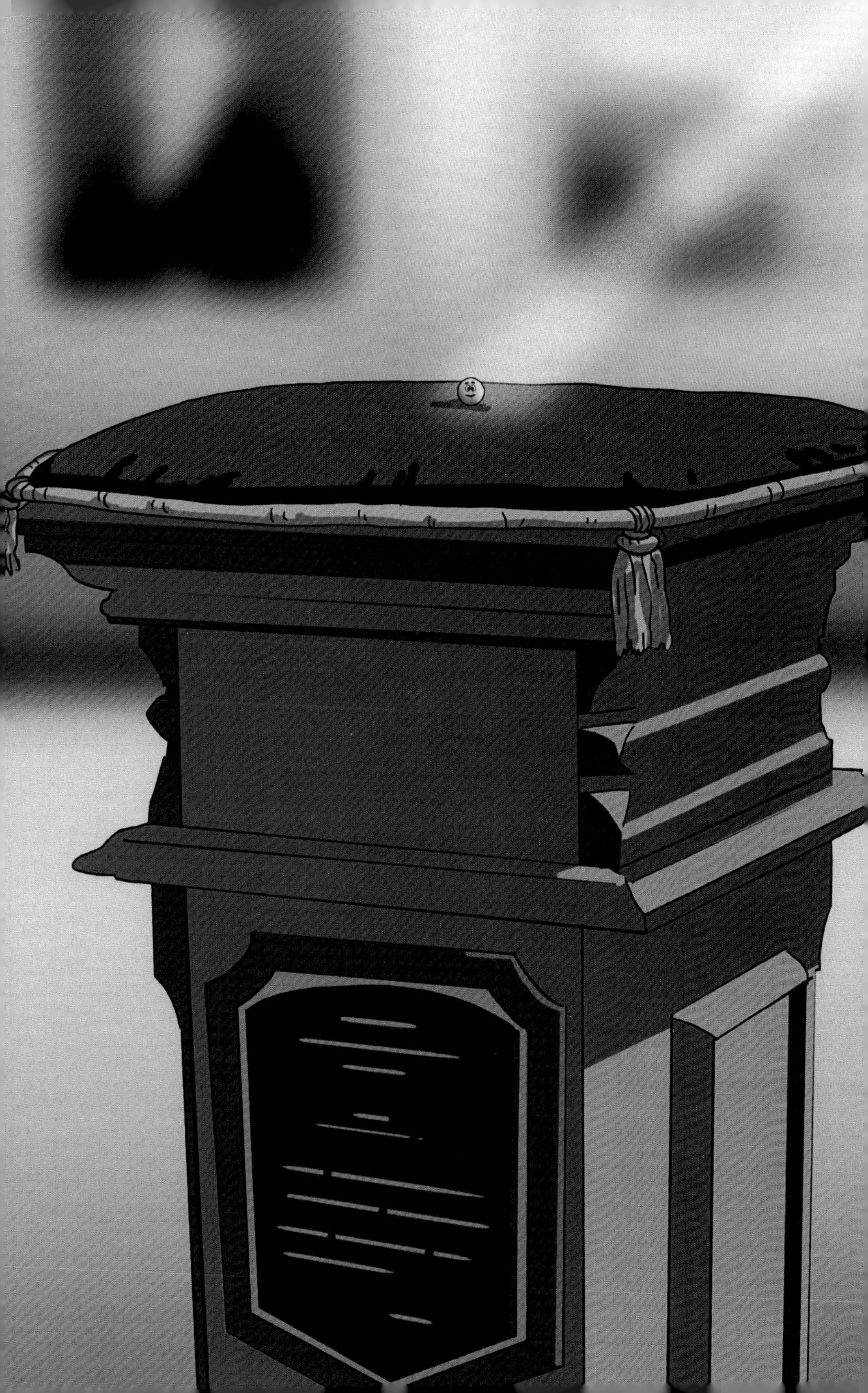

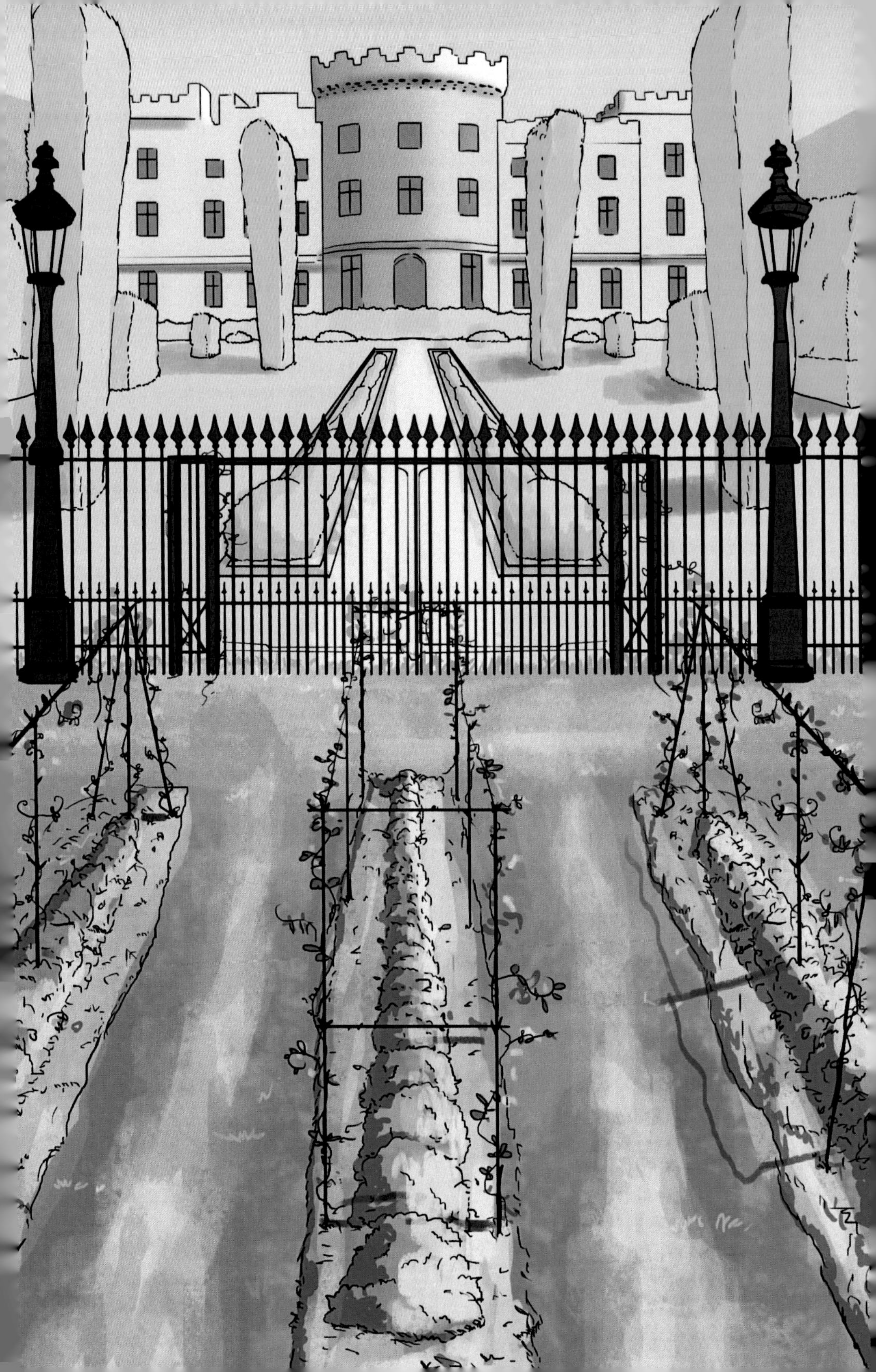

Peas are just like everyone else. They are born and schooled in their pods, and they strive to have a purpose. There are many jobs peas strive for—ranging from the best and most important peas becoming part of the royal pea soup to the most plain ones becoming boring side dishes for the commoners. The unlucky ones become food for animals or squashed. This story is about one pea in particular— Arthur Green.

The Greens lived in the farm right outside of the castle. In fact, you could see the royal garden through the fence that separated them. They were the boring side dish type. The Greens were a family of nine—dad Remus; mom Elizabeth; three girls Mary, Molly, and Rowan; and four boys Jonathan, Thomas, Virgil, and Arthur.

Arthur, being the youngest, loved to daydream about being something more than a side dish. He would stare through the fence and just let his imagination take him on adventures. Since he was always staring through the fence, he caught the servant's chatter about what was going on in the castle. Recently the castle was all abuzz about how the prince wanted to marry a princess, but not just any princess; she had to be a real princess.

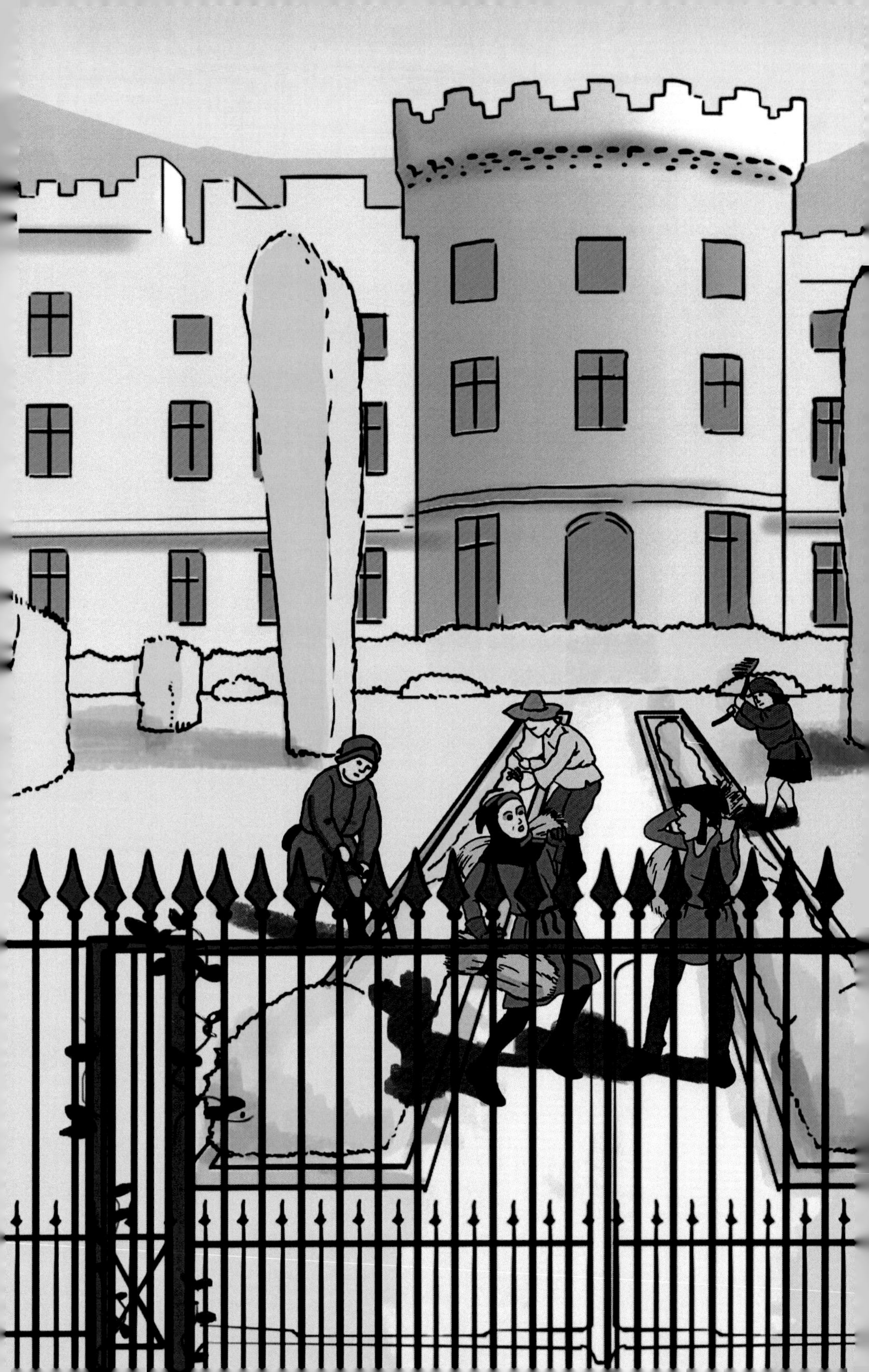

Everyday Arthur would rush to the fence to
see if he could hear if the prince had found his
princess. Each day it would be the same news.
The prince would send word that he had met
a princess, but there was always something
not quite right about her. He had traveled
the whole world and was very discouraged.
He wasn't sure how to tell if they were real
princesses.

One day, in the middle of the staff discussing the prince's latest letter, Arthur noticed the family who tended to his garden coming toward the peapods. Suddenly, there was a trumpet. It was the prince coming home. The family stopped to watch the prince enter the royal gates. Arthur noticed the royal staff stopping to watch the prince too.

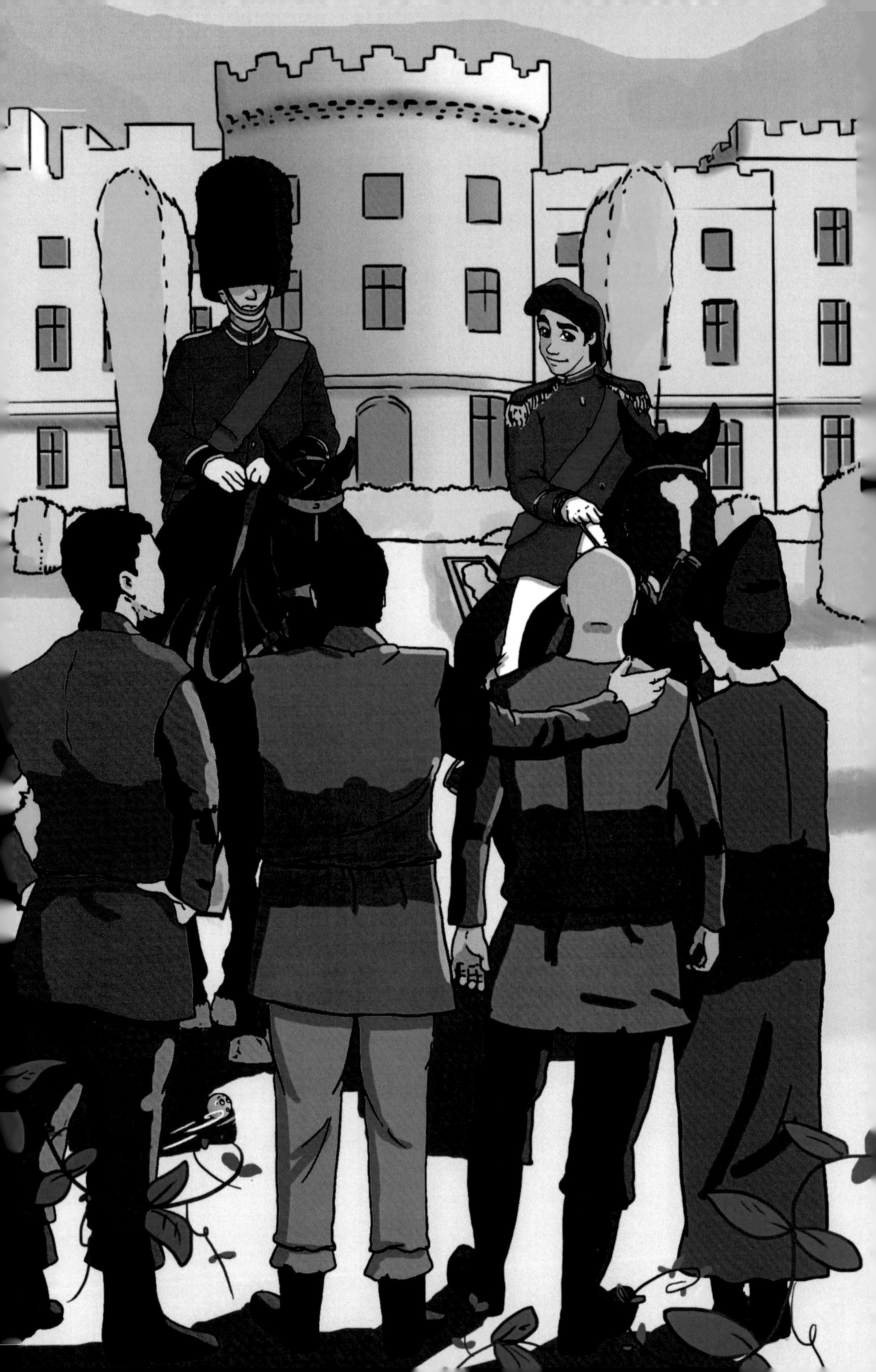

Arthur felt this is his chance to escape the life he felt he wasn't meant for. He backed up and rolled as fast as he could down the vine, and when he reached the end, he closed his eyes and leaped...and landed right into the royal gardener's basket of peas. He yelled a quick good-bye and I love you to his family as the gardener picked up the basket and headed into the castle's kitchen.

Arthur couldn't believe he was in the castle
kitchen! Everyone was racing around, trying to
get the prince's welcome-home feast ready and
talking about how the prince still hadn't found
a princess to marry. Arthur wasn't quite ready
to be part of the royal pea soup. He wanted
to know if the prince will ever find a princess,
so he rolled out of the basket and hid behind
some flour bags.

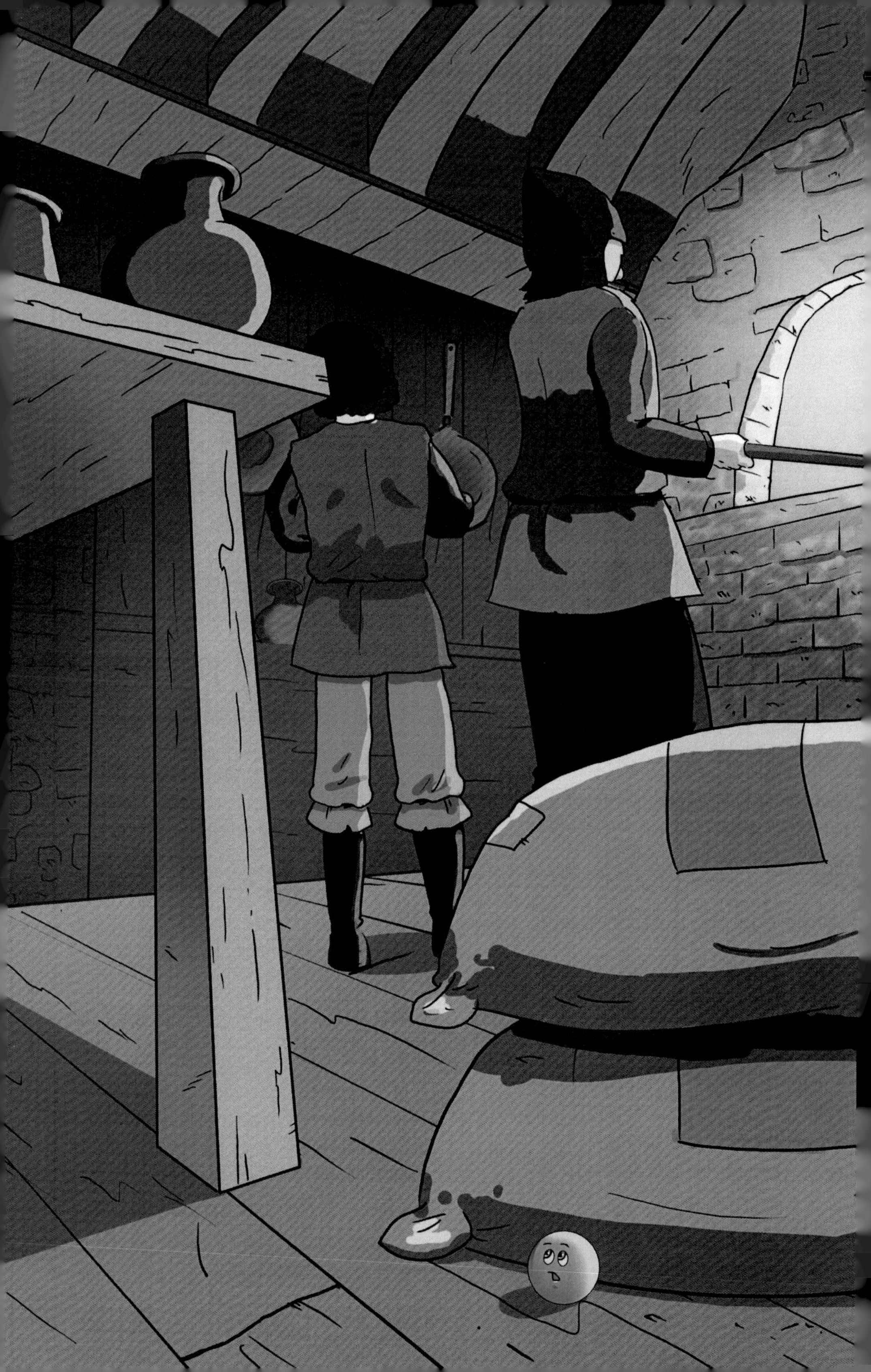

For days he hid behind the flour, just watching and listening to everything. One stormy night, the queen came into the kitchen. She was pacing around, thinking very hard. She was mumbling to herself, but Arthur couldn't tell what she was saying. He rolled out onto the counter to hear her better. "She says she is a real princess. How do I know she is a real princess and not some girl just trying to get a night out of the rain or trying to get my precious boy?" the queen mumbled. Suddenly she stood straight up and frantically looked around the kitchen. "We'll soon find out," the queen said as she grabbed Arthur.

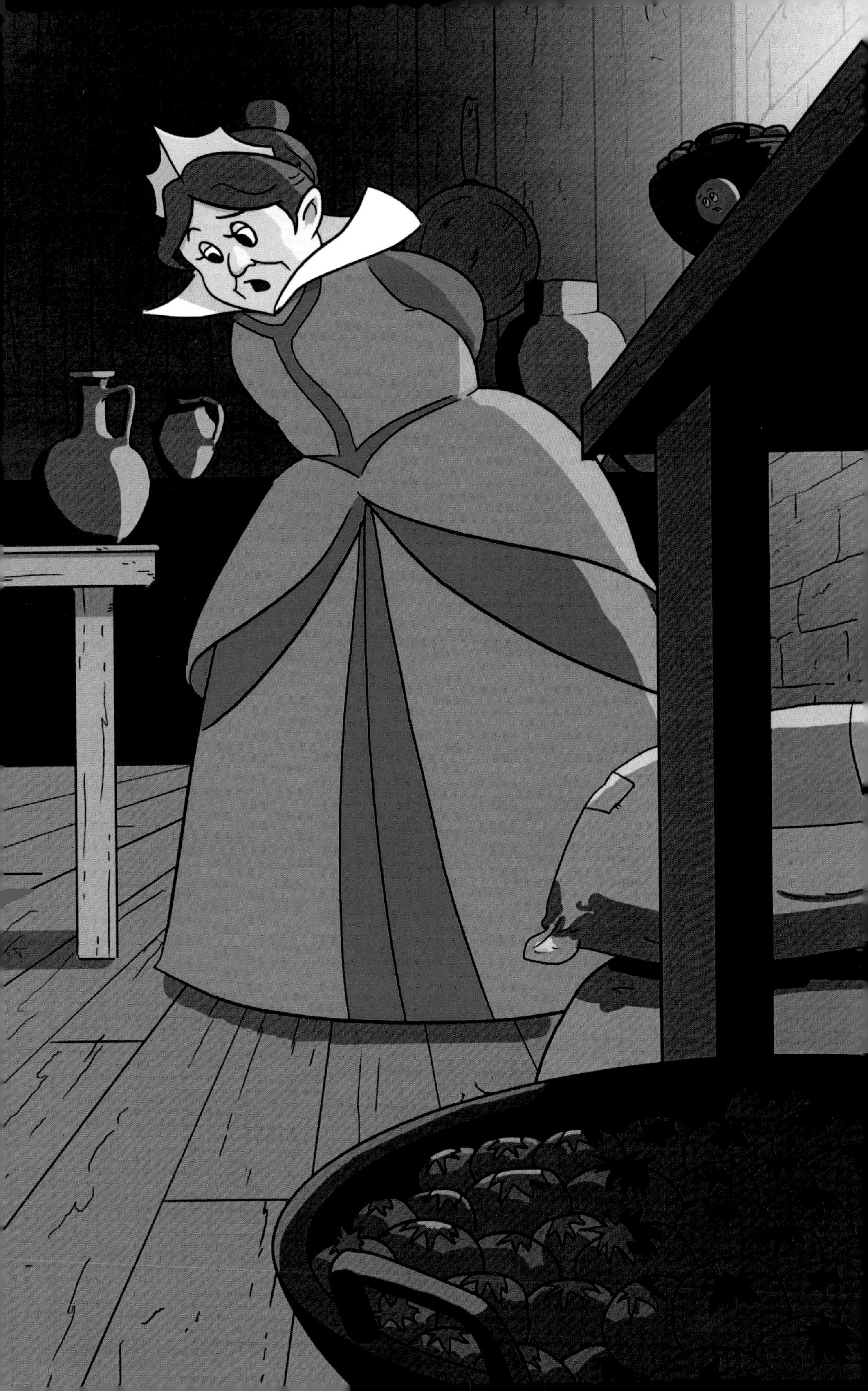

She walked straight to the bedchamber and
stripped the bed. She put a very stunned and
confused Arthur on the bottom of the bed.
She then placed twenty mattresses and twenty
eiderdown feather beds on top of Arthur. The
princess was to sleep on top of all of this, and
so she tried. Both the princess and Arthur
tossed and turned all night. The princess
couldn't get comfortable, and Arthur was
terrified; he was going to get squished. Every
time he would find a spot he felt was safe, the
princess would move. He could not figure out
why the queen had put him in the
princess's bed.

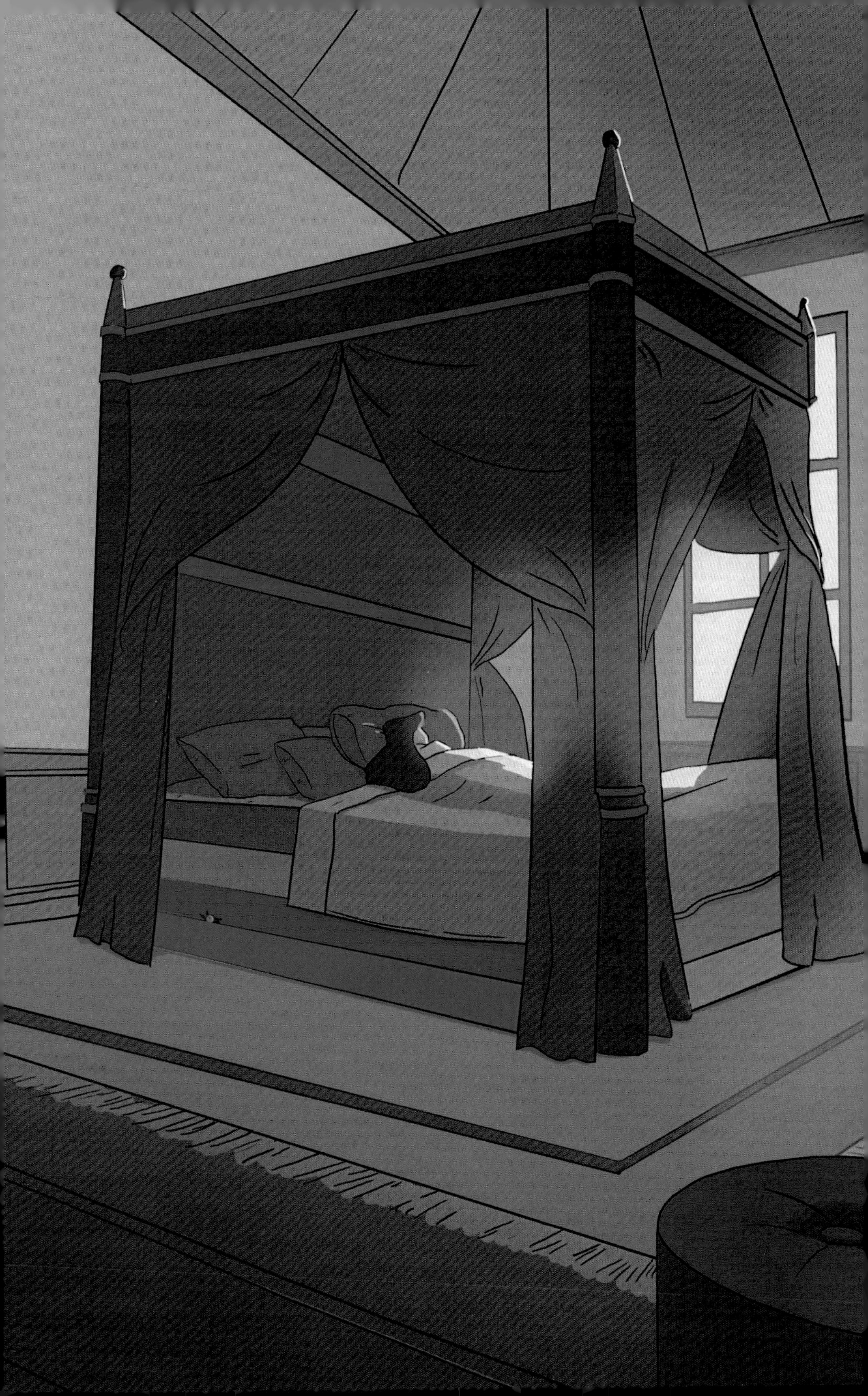

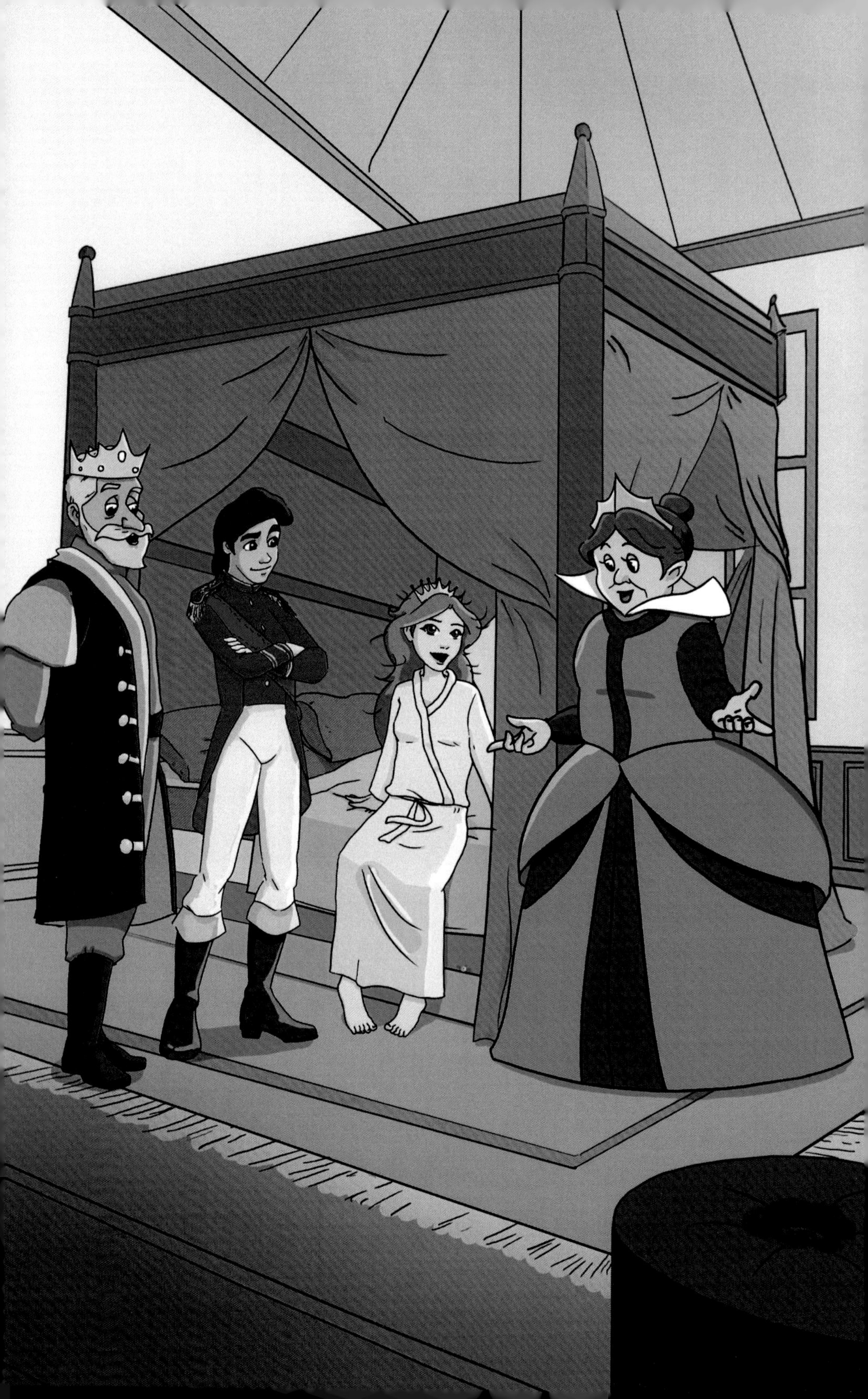

Finally it was morning, and Arthur heard a much-muffled royal family asking the princess how she slept. She told them she didn't sleep well and how there must be something in the bed because she was covered in bruises. The next part was very confusing to Arthur. The royal family sounded happy with the princess's response. Then the queen removed Arthur from the bed and told the princess that she and the prince must get married at once because she must be a real princess if she could feel a pea through all that bedding.

They did get married soon after. As for
Arthur, he was put in a museum to live there
for the rest of time.

"I sure was! Come see me anytime. And that
is how I became the most important pea of
all time—even more important
than a royal pea soup."

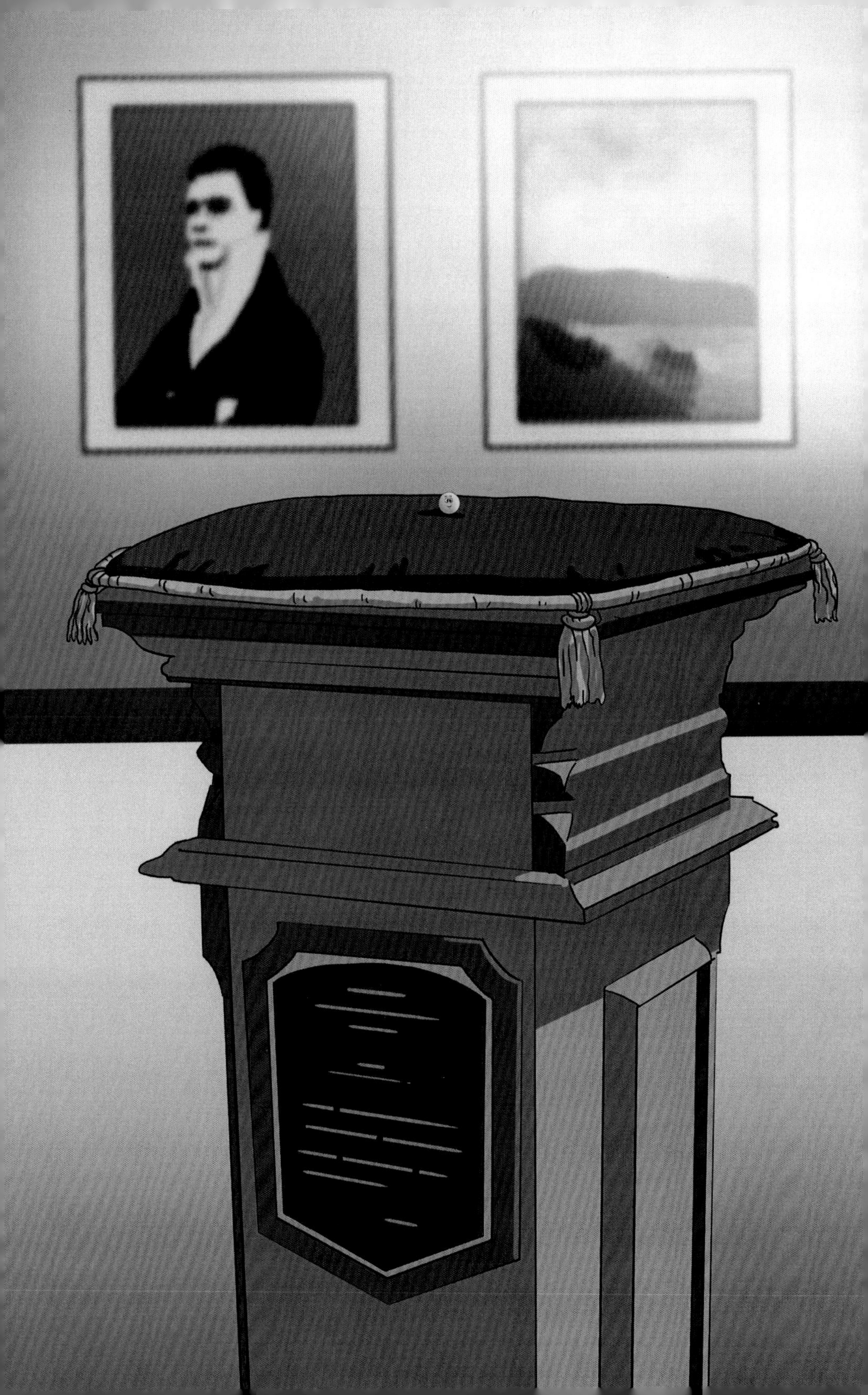

⊖|LIVE

---

listen|imagine|view|experience

AUDIO BOOK DOWNLOAD INCLUDED WITH THIS BOOK!

In your hands you hold a complete digital entertainment package. In addition to the paper version, you receive a free download of the audio version of this book. Simply use the code listed below when visiting our website. Once downloaded to your computer, you can listen to the book through your computer's speakers, burn it to an audio CD or save the file to your portable music device (such as Apple's popular iPod) and listen on the go!

How to get your free audio book digital download:

1. Visit www.tatepublishing.com and click on the e|LIVE logo on the home page.
2. Enter the following coupon code:
   66fa-19b4-b1f1-645e-2052-0f19-dd30-fd38
3. Download the audio book from your e|LIVE digital locker and begin enjoying your new digital entertainment package today!